Dear Parents:

Congratulations! Your child is taking the first steps on an exciting journey. The destination? Independent reading!

STEP INTO READING® will help your child get there. The program offers five steps to reading success. Each step includes fun stories and colorful art or photographs. In addition to original fiction and books with favorite characters, there are Step into Reading Non-Fiction Readers, Phonics Readers and Boxed Sets, Sticker Readers, and Comic Readers—a complete literacy program with something to interest every child.

Learning to Read, Step by Step!

Ready to Read   Preschool–Kindergarten
• big type and easy words • rhyme and rhythm • picture clues
For children who know the alphabet and are eager to begin reading.

Reading with Help   Preschool–Grade 1
• basic vocabulary • short sentences • simple stories
For children who recognize familiar words and sound out new words with help.

Reading on Your Own   Grades 1–3
• engaging characters • easy-to-follow plots • popular topics
For children who are ready to read on their own.

Reading Paragraphs   Grades 2–3
• challenging vocabulary • short paragraphs • exciting stories
For newly independent readers who read simple sentences with confidence.

Ready for Chapters   Grades 2–4
• chapters • longer paragraphs • full-color art
For children who want to take the plunge into chapter books but still like colorful pictures.

STEP INTO READING® is designed to give every child a successful reading experience. The grade levels are only guides; children will progress through the steps at their own speed, developing confidence in their reading.

Remember, a lifetime love of reading starts with a single step!

Step into Reading, Random House, and the Random House colophon are registered trademarks of Penguin Random House LLC.

Visit us on the Web!
StepIntoReading.com
rhcbooks.com

Educators and librarians, for a variety of teaching tools, visit us at RHTeachersLibrarians.com

ISBN 978-1-9848-4784-3 (trade) — ISBN 978-1-9848-4785-0 (lib. bdg.)

Printed in the United States of America

10 9 8 7 6 5 4 3 2 1

nick jr.
TOP WING

THE HAUNTED CAVE

by Christy Webster

based on the teleplay "The Mystery
of the Haunted Cave" by Scott Kraft

illustrated by Dave Aikins

Random House 🏠 New York

Brody and Rod
go into the woods
with Bea.
They want to earn
camping badges!

Bea starts a fire.
Rod and Brody
make popcorn.
As they eat,
Bea tells
a spooky story.

It is about a cave.
There are ghosts
inside the cave!

Nearby,
Baddy and Betty
smell the popcorn.
Baddy wants some!
He howls to scare
the cadets away.

Rod and Brody

hear the spooky sound.

They are nervous.

Bea puts out the fire.
She and the cadets think
the sound
is coming from
a haunted cave.

They find the cave.

The cadets are brave.

They go inside!

Baddy flies
into the cave.
He wants to scare
the cadets even more!
He bangs on
an old cart.

Baddy moans
like a ghost!
Rod and Brody
are scared.

Oh, no!
Baddy's cart
gets loose.
It speeds
through the cave!
Baddy screams.

Brody flies
to save him,
but he cannot
stop the cart!
It goes even faster.

Rod calls
his Road Wing.

Rod chases the cart.
He uses his claw
to slow it down.

The cart stops
just in time.
Brody and Baddy
are safe!

The cadets
help Baddy
out of the cave.
They see
Betty and Bea.

The cave
is not haunted
after all!

Baddy says he is sorry
for scaring the cadets.
Rod, Brody, and Bea
share their popcorn.

But there will be

no more ghost stories!

Hooray!
Rod and Brody
earn their camping
badges!